ELECTION DAY

Election Day

Election Day is a special day when people go to vote and choose their leaders. It happens on the first Tuesday after the first Monday in November. On this day, people decide who will be the President, Senators, Representatives, and other important officials. Voting on Election Day helps make sure everyone has a say in how the country is run.

Sammy and Aunt Emma

Sammy was an eager and curious eight-year-old who loved spending time with his Aunt Emma. One morning, she came over for breakfast with some exciting news. "Sammy, today is Election Day!" she said cheerfully. Sammy tilted his head, confused. "What's Election Day, Aunt Emma?" he asked. "It's the day we choose who will make important decisions for our town!"

VOTE

Aunt Emma explained, "Voting is when people choose leaders, like a mayor or president, who will help make the rules for our town or country." Sammy's eyes widened with excitement. "Do you get to pick the leaders? That sounds so cool!" Aunt Emma nodded, "Yes! And today, I'll show you exactly how it's done!"

Sammy was buzzing with curiosity as Aunt Emma grabbed her purse. "Are we going to vote right now?" he asked eagerly. Aunt Emma smiled and said, "Yes! We're going to the voting station together. You'll see how grown-ups make their choices." Sammy rushed to put on his shoes, excited for this new adventure.

The Polling Station

When they arrived at the polling station, Sammy saw a lot of people waiting in line. There were friendly faces everywhere, and Sammy felt the excitement in the air. "This is where people come to vote!" Aunt Emma said. Sammy watched closely as people took turns going into little booths, wondering what happened inside.

As they moved closer to the booths, Aunt Emma explained, "Each person gets a ballot, just like this one, and they go inside the booth to choose who they think will be the best leader." Sammy could see people coming out of the booths with happy faces, proudly wearing stickers that said "I Voted!" He couldn't wait to see what the booths were like up close.

VOTE
RIGHT!
VOTE!
VOTE!

When it was Aunt Emma's turn, she handed over her name and received a ballot. "Now it's time to vote!" she said. Sammy watched as she disappeared behind the curtain into the voting booth. He imagined what it was like inside, thinking about how grown-ups made such important decisions in private.

VOTE

Learning About Ballots

After Aunt Emma finished voting, she walked out of the booth with a smile on her face and showed Sammy her "I Voted!" sticker. "This is what you get after voting," she said proudly. Sammy's eyes lit up. "That's so cool! I want to vote when I grow up!" Aunt Emma chuckled, "You will, Sammy, and it's an important job."

I VOTED!
I VOTED!

At home, Aunt Emma explained more about the ballot. She showed Sammy an old sample ballot and pointed to the names of the candidates. "This is how you vote. You check the box next to the name of the person you think will do the best job." Sammy thought it was fun, like solving a puzzle.

Sammy tried filling in the pretend ballot, carefully marking his choice. "There! I voted!" he said proudly, showing it to Aunt Emma. She smiled and said, "Great job, Sammy! Voting is how you help make sure the right people are chosen to make decisions." Sammy beamed, feeling like he had just done something really important.

Why Voting Matters

Emily woke up early on Election Day, filled with excitement. She put on a special outfit that her parents had bought for her, and they all had a big breakfast together. Today was the day they would participate in something very important.

As they walked to the polling station, Emily noticed many of her neighbors were also heading to vote. Some were chatting excitedly, and others waved hello. Emily felt a sense of unity, knowing everyone was coming together for a common purpose.

vote!

At the polling station, Emily watched as her parents voted. She felt proud to be part of a family that valued their role in democracy. Even though she was too young to vote, Emily knew that one day, she would have her turn to make her voice heard.

QUIZ

Circle the correct answer

Who did Sammy spend Election Day with?

a) His mom

b) His friend Mia

c) His Aunt Emma

What did Aunt Emma show Sammy at the breakfast table?

a) A sample ballot

b) A voting sticker

c) A map of the polling station

Where did Sammy and Aunt Emma go to vote?

a) The grocery store

b) The polling station

c) The park

What did people receive after voting?

a) A certificate

b) A medal

c) An "I Voted!" sticker

What did Sammy dream about at the end of the story?

a) Becoming a teacher

b) Voting when he grows up

c) Traveling to space

Made in the USA
Coppell, TX
11 November 2024

39639635R00021